François Szabó

Enigmatic Sound

Obsidiana Press
obsidianapress.net

François Szabó

Enigmatic Sound

Obsidiana Press
obsidianapress.net

ISBN 978-1-948114-20-2

Printed in the United States of America.

Obsidiana Press

obsidianapress.net

info@obsidianapress.net

oplibros@aol.com

To Carole and our Magnificent Five:
Dimitri, Lili, Rafael, Tanya and Vega

How you see my love

The time is now to know

How to make the present better

You know I'm not waiting

I'm writing in the water

I'm writing in your skin

Such a love can do it for us

I know you truly love again

Like all these days

It's not a foolish game

It's never a game

It's life

It's our story

It's our world

In the laps of time to live

We must make all better

And certainly meet us forever

Like unforgivable lovers

November 22 / 2017

Montpellier

This sand is the part of fine particle of beach

'Cause we send stars in the sky

like transform the earth ball

In a fountain of joy happy to love and live

The sun shining in the eyes of water globus

The hair in the hand of spirit

And the skin tender to the cool wind

We have in the nacre the sky of the sea

The pearl is something renewed

And so the lent crescent fine pellicular peal

Is for us a celestial vision

And we need something else

Like a palm of my hand where you orange

Let up the sky open blooming

The wings of brave day is now like everyday

And our love is growing like the plant-tree of life

And the tenderness of the spirit fire

Is up up to the heart

The river moon of gifts

Dreams all around

Reality leave of mint

And sunshine every word

A precise way of the love

Set up set each day

Forever in the bath of felicity

Unexpected

1

Something like a drop
A place nearby
And the dream
Of wonderful day

2

Take this piece of Earth
This rock sandstone
Or the leaves
Growing on the ground

3

If I can't tell you why
Don't worry
It's because of madness
Or ill respiration

4

But don't let this rock
In his loneliness
Maybe a laugh
Maybe spell a word

5

The summer is the fire
Of burning days
Of sick vegetation
Of a scare's time

6

The same old sentences
I can't try a new way
I'm not able to wonder
All my life I mean

7

On the hill
The edge
Is only a vision
True-false vision

Dream On!

If you can see the paradise's flame

Even when you despair for the future

If you say me something unusual

-like something new, happy and full of peace.

If you can tell me a calm warm weather

And built the house and let grow the tree

Where the friendship is the edge of all languages

So my friend –all humanity- we will change a lot the world

'Cause with you, Oh paradise bird! All the way is wide open

And I hear you all the day and all the night

You're singing the flowers' song

Like a Magnolia on the rising day

With the new peace vision

And the gift on your heart.

24/07/2017

Montpellier (France)

Carole my love
It's too high
It's not hard
It's just truth
Carole my love
I dream
Like à stream
Of the ocean
Carole my love
It's our way
Following
The milky way.

Montpellier
November 18, 2017
23h30

I can't understand

I'm not here

In the such place I need

Do you know what's happen?

To love each other

And waiting for such a good life

And writing our love everyday

'Cause we can't do anything other

Whatever the day

Whatever the time

We are dreaming and living in love

Remembering the same old things

And the recent meeting

Now the sun is shining for us

For our hearts

For the way we need

And learning to see each footstep

We know how our love is

And we think how to transcend our life.

Montpellier
November 19/2017

To say never the same way

The same love for you

Change the verses

Since change the senses

The blue blue sunny sky

In our heads

Now it's time to meet again

'Cause you know it

Love can wait

But presence it's wood on fire

And the diamond shines

But perish on flames

Diamond eternal love

We need to preserve it

And we have it in our hearts

November 19/2017
Montpellier

Who loves knows how happy is

Who have someone to love

Need no more than this

Carole you're in my life

Like each world's element

It's an all earth and sky

A story river with gathering

At the sea of beatitude

You're the one I need

And I know how much

You love really

Take care of you dear

Like I take care of me

And the way will be wide open

For us forever

November 19/2017

Montpellier

Whatever the day
Whatever the night
The new sunshine of our love
Is one an all eternity's shining time
'Cause you're all in and over me
'Cause you're waiting for me
We can explore only tenderness
And learning the light always
We meet both love and happiness
In this renewed love story

November 19/ 2017
Montpellier

Open your eyes

Through the shadows

A light is shining

It's your eyes

It's your love so deep

It's fire inside

It's health to win

The night comes

But the stars still remain the same

Your world is mine

My world is yours

And our love

Still burning and turning

Like galaxy

Opens the great days

November 22 /2017

Montpellier

Imagine my dear

Walking along

The « Nombre d'or » place

Walking in the December day

By night too

'Cause it's a such nice place

'Cause the lights are magic

'Cause you and me seem a kind of miracle

'Cause we need it again and again

'Cause with everyday it's joy

And too we know really how we need

To live each day and night

It's like to built our lives

It's like to make real a dream

03/12/2017

Montpellier

The night comes

But your eyes are shining

Like the most brilliant diamonds

I know how much you love

Like a star can burning

Like in the sky

Somewhere to turn the face

And now and here

I'm telling you

With or without you

That you will be here this week

And that I'm sure we will be very happy

Happiest again living our dream

An orange in the hand

A place near me

And my heart like a pulsar

03/12/2017

Montpellier

And yours every time everywhere

For you Carole my woman fear

For you my spiritual verse

For you my renewed life

My dear Carole

A love song like a little twinkle star

A love song like birds in your head

And the song of our way since a very very long time ago

And this place where I'll nevermore will be lying

'Cause you know it I will survive with this story

'Cause you know it I will your planet or doblestar with you

It's happens here and now and this room this apartment

You know it like The place where we have to be

And where all is a golden circle of time

03/12/2017

Montpellier

This day it's a day without hours

All the things late and strange

I don't know why this mute day

Is again a distortion in the life

All the joy of love is truth

And it's now possible to live again

'Cause we know truly what is the way

'Cause we know that my soul is in you

'Cause we say the wide open space

And before the night our day is not finished

Our luminescent smile and the feeling of love

Up up in the sky like stars in the sky

You stand here by me near me

In my heart like living strength

Now I have to renew the verse

The poetry can be

Each day and night

Make the future

And let our lives cool and marvelous

You know it we have the consciousness of love

And never forget to shine along the way

Our time is to be

Our time is forever

Our time is still and diamond

 If you can see me forever

You know that all is yours

I know what you want

And I try to write the bird song

For you again and again

Flowers and tenderness of the skin

Hair and our communication

Like the morning song in the night

That wake up our love like the sun can make for the earth

And rivers and rivers singing in our heads

In our minds like a water of living road

The mountains of strength help us

And our love is more and more than the eight-star

We can all along the day make sense and light

In the night a calm respiration with tenderness

Let us to give the near day to be

And to continue these words for us

Between a light and a sunrise

Between flower and trifle

Between you and me

The space is off

Only love and love again

Like all we need

Joining our souls in the right way

We enjoy to be love-human beings

The time is shining in our dreams like a star

You know it well we tell our story

And now learning to wait our new hour

We keep smile and joy in our heart

We need tenderness and calm love

Hope you're well now between the day off

and the day open

Our way is to be

And walking along the street of destiny

The city call us

We need to be in love forever

We need to meet felicity together

And our way is wide open

Take care of your way

Be the sun always

I 'll be your intimacy for ever

I let the past for ever

And you know I am not waiting

I just want to know a new vision

The same old vision of future to imagine

You make me happy always you know

And the strength will be mine over the health

'Cause you know better to live

'Cause you know better to live

Than disappear in the hole of unconsciousness

I'll never try better to live than in love for you

'Cause you know it was always that

My life is on our word on your lips

My life is on the presence of your shinning eyes

Always be that I can believe it

'Cause you know always be the same

Your name is mine a heart my heart

I can't live without it

Easy to understand

Without water without sun

My life can't grow

Earth needs you

But never tell you more than these words

Do what you feel

Always be free

I'll live happy

I'll be a tree

I'm in love with you

The night never comes you always shines

You are the star that leads my way

You are all for me

Sphere of the universe

The endless happiness

In the Milky Way

The tree's strength

The telluric force

The vegetal tenderness

The water kindness

The sky pure sky

My respiration

You are

Orange in my blue words

You are

The scum of all the waves

When I see you coming in love

When you stay too

You are this flower

Who blooms everyday

All the time your eyes in my eyes

The both wings
The air on silent wave
The gold ring

We know our tale
All the road we made
Is on the way

Sent all our messages
Paper's poems
Flying like blue bird In love song

Where the dreams are reality
We can wide open our eyes

Now imagine us
Really truly
Now imagine us
In the earth all sunny
In that place here
Town of happiness
Where all happens

And we staying together

All the day all the night

Making sense

All we need happens

Our life is not an isle

All near the sea with blue lagunas

Near mountains in harmony with the sky

I tell you the same things

In our apartments

In our millenary city

We need each other

My brain and your

Drawing our future

On the sunny light of our destiny

Can you sing me your felicity ?

I can hear you all the day

But you needn't sing all the time

You are free to do all you want

And me too so I need to show you

Everyday writing my love poems

You can see me like you want

I hear now birds who send me your message

I want your human voice too in this eternal life

Like you need my voice

Can you show me your face often or everyday?

I am happy with you for ever

You know you have to see me too

'Cause you will never loose me

'Cause I will never loose you

We are golden ring

Dense floor of my land

Rocks and

Sand along our river of Eternity

Roots trees looking for strength

My leaves tell you

How you are sweet tender Carole

Each drop on my leaves

A kiss

I am not

A fish of

desire

I can call you

Everywhere

When you need

So, you, in a blue dream comin'

So, in the sweet wave on our river of Eternity

My leaf leads you to me

'Cause you are behind the front door

of my apartment

And comin' in only if you want

François for you

Sounds of life

Then over the day and the night

Our love persist resist always

Cause Carole is a heroine

Cause our story is so beautiful

Cause the way is wide open

For us two together

And I think on the orange sun and earth

I remember of Saturn and rings

I remember of ears lost than renew soon I hope

Our harmonic relation full of passion

Humor and simplicity natural

Come on to celebrate our love

Each time possible easier

On the cords of your voice

The night never happens

It's always day for us

And light so light !

13/08/2018

Poems to resist

For Carole

July 2018

The shape of the world
On my own deep soul
Is so different of my dream
That I can't tell you why

Now the sun never set
Cause of your love forever
I'm so grateful for that all
And never asleep in another country

My dear Carole full of love
Can you imagine our lives now
When the day past again and again
Never forget the past forge the future

08/07/2018

How do you feel sweet ?

Have you time enough to hear me ?

09/07/2018

Dream after dream along the pain

Signs after signs along again

I left again my hope for you

I'm right to find your heart

Cause you are mine it's true

10/07/2018

Dearest strong enough to say

All the day open for us

And singing all the song of humanity

Standing singing on

Let the sun shine again

11/07/2018

Among the kind of pleasure freedom
I think of you like a leaf flying
Over and over to find the river of eternity
I let from the past regards torpe beings
And make a new way for us together

11/07/2018

Thinking about reality

It's all a shame this way

When false men and women

Try to forget the human being

The last call of the life

11/07/2018

Dreaming again and again
Life open in my own soul
Try my dear Carole to understand
Our solitude standing over that way
Cause better say truth always

11/07/2018

Later or sooner the ring of consciousness
Tell us to find another our way
You're happy face full of joy
Is a happy ending for me

Like was she were
Never woman can be
I'm so hopefull
To have you in my arms
That the day begins fine

And so on come on darling
Take this hand mine like you always want
And let the sun shine in your mean
For a new age empire of tenderness
Now always in yours eyes
I see my life really
Cause of my faith in a word
That word is only love

Jeudi 09h 12/07/2018 pavillon le Guilhem

O dearest ! full of happiness !
The micocoulier tree send you this message
I'm writing in the hospital again
Trying to renew our dignity

This song is a heaven song
A man's song in love
I'm in love with you
Acer can be my name
You know it truly

La Grisette is your reality
Regliss and honey only
Montpellierenca like me
Our spot is here in this city

And our sons and girls
Have to know this story
It's so important like word
First word of life

12/07/2018 09h15 Montpellier le Guilhem

Hope or despair it depends
It depends of me at all
The day never says without light
If I can tell sincerely and honestly

It's time walking another
Step on step on go ahead !
Each inch it's a pulse mine
Each meter it's a big word
Each kinetic it's a poem

You try to find excuse for me
Don'try please, I didn't
I have to prove my love for you
Again this day more again

Audience this day
A great day for reality
My own presence stand by you
In the city of Montpellier

God's event it's not an evidence

We are human beings it's the first

We need only true love and happiness

Never other things

Vendredi 13/07/2018 07h20

Oh happy day ! I hope ! (Samedi 14/07/2018)

Shades shades clouds and clouds
I have to return indoor
The time is now to realize
Something new unattempt

The day is blooming like you
Every day our doble star know that
If you can say help
I'll try any way to go with
Cause you know you are one

The shine of my body set off
I need to incent the light
Another way another morning
Cause it's two our reality

We live for beauty truly
For tenderness between us
Us Is the word of Open
Is our's too now

The links of souls
Is like night fishing
A "Line, live in the sounds
Then throw silvery nounces" (Derek Walcott)

16/07/2018
8h

A kind of loneliness this morning
The facts are stronger than my life
I need something new like a light in despair
We try to exchange our feelings every days

These words are longing in time
But now is my open mouth
This statue is non stop
The way can't stop
On the finish line

But these verse so empty
So full of love too
Hard in hope of love too
Hard in hope of love too

Do you think else more ?
Don't that so !
The way is unhappy
But the finish is the top

I send messages for you

Cause you're my girl-wife

Cause you're are all for me

The Goddess of Love

Wednesday 18/07/2018

09h02

Morning call of nature
Birds singing'
Tree quiet murmuring
And sun not yet on

The paradise is not late
Rest in pace son of love
Human love each other
And delight sentiments
For really oldness

The rain drop don't fall
In the joy of word
Is found another
For renew again

The deep helpness
To respire wide
On this summer
Of the hot volcano

Here we are

In few of our destiny

Since deep I hope

Always together

20/07/2018

If the canopy can memorize the world

The sun shines not only for humanity

The way of love is wide eternity

That never ends

The smell of leaves benefic

Are all for you Carole

All my universe is your's

For ever for our lives

Endless story

Can you try to write unusual this main ?

The wings on learning on you

To know if we are courageous

And also beings healthy

Now the remote control

Is fail by ignorance

Only love and intelligence

Help us

Where the two loves

Carole François are

This is always

Now

11h 21/07/2018 le Guilhem

More for Carole

Yet published in Cant per Carole paper book

After a long way
We need to find
Our paradise
Your face is shinning
In it always

"Bright Star"

Keats

O my Star in the Space-Tree
Of my life
Sun who lead me
Bright Star
I heard your voice this morning
What a high pleasure !
Love can make me happy
And I was it so tenderly
Leaves of my being
Help me to know
All Kindness
All Details
All Precision

All Nuances

The sound of your voice
It's of a bird's song
It's a soul expression
It's a living world
It's your truth

Precision clock
But with a just sense
With full generosity
With strong imagination
You lead all
All your lives

In our city
I see all the light
Light of passion
Near the sea
Near the mountains
Near of all we need

I am
Oak in love
Montpellier's Acer
With the water song
You are my
Flower of joy
Among your luxuriant vegetation
On benefic earth

Our footprints
Don't let imagine

All our secret lover's life
Violet dreamy you were

So long way
To send us
Together
In a life wide open

"I never dream to remember"
Dave Brinks

In my mind
All is to imagine
Our future
All my life is this
And love is our way
Drawing projects
Writing our lives
Spelling our names
Telling our vision

One vision

My arms embrace
Your world
Infinite world
I want always
Laurel for you Carole

"Calling your name"
Dave Brinks

Running to you
All the day
All the night
Between sunset
And new sunrise
Every day
Is my resurrection
Dreaming to be phenix

Writing on the soul's skin

Writing on paper's skin

Writing on leaves

Writing on computer's wave

Writing on skin deep

Making verses on scum

Making verses on heart

Making verses on flower

Making verses on sky

So only making verses on you

My lips spell your name

And the wind

Looks for you

But we needn't the wind

You know my love

All is certain

My Poem is

Always the key

Of you heart

Blue devotion words

Carole always
Orange in my verses
And our love
Gold

Poem on
Paper's flower
Rose
On this day

Fabulous Way

December 28 2019

Yet published in review on line *Nueva Ola*

The time comes

To write these words

Full of joy and happiness

When the love gives

When the love dares

And when the wind

Blows on the land

On the leaves

Writing short poems

Natural poems

In god's tongue

Shaking like a leaf

Some sounds of poetry.

Flying upon the trees

Aerial sense of lightness

Divine bird's songs

Sending a message

To always renew love

Sweet and tender

Like everyday

Kinetic poem

Chosen by me

To conquer you

Again and again

Among the streets

Mine is a magic one

Where infinites possibilities grow

Where to come is evidence

And where we are in peace

Politic chessboard

Poetic translation

Walls of books

Library cathedral

to hide lovers

Some meat for holidays

To spend the weeks.

Spread wide wings

To support the sky

Blue blue sky of Montpellier

Always the sun shining

A delicate vision

Full of beauty

Full entertainment

Like a child's game

So real so serious

Searching happiness

By association

Between words and visions.

Sending hope and favorable days
Spelling your name like devotion
Understanding that never will be other one
Than you in this time in the giant space
And that at the sea always return the water
So the new wave is a vision
In movement of scum singing
Up the wave recreated
Wave upon wave
On the book of sand
Ripple marks of all eternity.

The Magnificent Five

To Carole and our Magnificent Five:

Dimitri, Lili, Rafael, Tanya and Vega

We like our Magnificent Five so clever and courageous.

We spent our life quiet and full of your tenderness and freedom it's thanks to you. It never happens disillusionment you give us strength all the day all the night. We feel happy well in love for you. Can we understand all your self-denial ? Now sure strong in this way this certainty sends us message of peace and resolution of strength and imagination always renewed.

Hey this is a moment of gratitude

Because all our life is a pleasure

Magical moments we spend thanks to you

So much so real so incredible

We want to care again and again

We want to say you the poetry's words

And feeling all the space full of happiness

Because you were and you are all for us

Better with you all

Great life in the middle of age

Be happy

See you soon !

Whether it be

On the air Rafael

Architectural Tanya and Lili

Life science Dimitri

Or poetry Vega

You are our

Magnificent Five

Afterword
By Roger West

François Szabo's aptly-titled latest collection of poems is another affirmation of his polyglot poetry. This collection is in English; to be precise it is not a translation into English, he has chosen to write these poems directly into English. It is no mean feat to write, and to write poetry, and to write good poetry in a non-native language. François follows in a tradition of poets and other writers who have made that choice: Vladimir Nabokov, Bharat Mukherjee, Salman Rushdie, George Szirtes. Whereas some writers have grappled with the wisdom of that choice and agonized about losing that 'domestic diction', that 'interior language', others have embraced it and sprinted off joyfully with the possibilities. François is definitely in this select group. Szirtes writes about the slide from the native to a non-native tongue and describes the poet "slightly detached from the soil you tread on...you see some things that the soil-born cannot." Poetry, he goes on "only appears at the point at which language is both familiar and strange." With François' poetry we see this exemplified and amplified; here is a writer - a "Montpellierenc" who moves between at least 5 languages.

Consider for example the lines "and so the lent crescent fine pellicular peal / is for us a celestial vision." Grammatically correct, yes; using words that exist, yes. But the choice of those words and their ordering is unusual and the strangeness of their juxtaposition gives an elusive quality to the text, the meaning hovering tantalizingly within reach but difficult to grasp. This elliptical daring coupled with the rolling assonance and sonority is what poetry is all about - vivid, provisional, unique and bizarre. It follows in the tradition of English mystics like Hopkins who used that tumble of off-kilter words to great effect: "her earliest stars, earl stars, stars principal overbend us, fire-featuring heaven." François' lines "Like was she were / Never woman can be" evoke earlier poets like Blake.

These poems, all dedicated to Carole and the children, have a thematic and tonal integrity which gives the collection a force. On first reading it has a cyclical quality; themes, images, words and phrases reappear, differently juxtaposed and rolling ever onwards, building towards crescendos then falling back. But then on further reading, this repetition becomes more like ripples radiating from the core. "I know what you want / And I try to write the bird song / For you again and again", he writes and this is what the collection becomes - a rewriting of a declaration of love over and over so that it takes on an organic life force of its own, ever-evolving and growing from its experiences and understandings. "In the laps of time to live / We must make all better / And certainly meet us forever / Like unforgivable lovers." Our ever-outward-flowing creativity and passion neatly encapsulated but with that elliptical sting in those last three words.

These are poems that are brave, honest and "wide open" - songs of renewal; renewal of love, of life, of the galaxy and the universe. And ultimately of a poetry that "makes the future."

Contents

―――

Unexpected /**11**

Poems to resist /**43**

More for Carole /**65**

Fabulous way /**75**

The magnificent five /**83**

Afterword by Roger West /**87**

BIBLIOGRAPHIE

Poésie (recueils)

- *La Bellesa,* ebook en catalan, Obsidiana Press, avril 2019 (accessible ici)

- *Cant per Carole*, version papier bilingue català / français, Obsidiana / États-Unis, 2018

- *Cant per Carole*, Obsidiana Press, livre électronique libre, 2018

- *Aster Carole*, Obsidiana Press, 2018

- *Mesclun*, poésie, Obsidiana Press / États-Unis, 2017

- *Visa Permanent*, Obsidiana Press, ebook gratuit, Etats-Unis, 2017

- *Au Finisterre de l'imagination*, poésie, Obsidiana Press / États-Unis, 2016

- *La double impression et autres poèmes,* Obsidiana Press / États-Unis, 2015

- *Une voix de parole et d'extase,* Société des poètes français / France, 2015

- *La primera frase es una pregunta / La première phrase est une question,* El Taller del poeta / Espagne, 2015

- *Again, Life is a Gift !* recueil de poems en anglais, publisher : HOLI, Bhubaneswar (India), septembre 2015

- *Nathanaël sous le figuier,* recueil de poèmes en français, peintures de Victorita Dutu, Obsidiana Press, Charleston WV, États-Unis, 2015, ebook gratuit

- *Résurgences,* poésie, livre d'artiste avec Monique Ariello, 3 exemplaires, 2014

- *Une teinte en retrait*, poésie, Obsidiana Press, 2013

- *Poemas Punk*, traduction en espagnol de Angeles Bustamante Gonzalez, Obsidiana Press, 2012

- *La Fraîcheur*, petits poèmes en prose, Obsidiana Press, 2012

- *La Fe : libreto de opera / la Foi*, livret d'opéra, réédition en ebook, Obsidiana Press, 2012

- *Non à la peste brune !* pamphlet. ebook, Obsidiana Press, 2012

- *Fragilitate de cisturi*, traduction en roumain de *Fragilité de cistes* par Ioana Trica, Editora Ex Libris Universalis, 2011

- *Planète Pacifiée*, poésie, Obsidiana Press, 2012, réédition en e-book, préface de Jean Joubert, encres de Dimitri Szabó

- *Punk Poems*, poésie, Obsidiana Press, 2011, VO en anglais

- *Nouvelles Stances à Lénotchka*, poésie, Obsidiana Press, 2011

- *Planète Pacifiée*, poésie, 2010, avec 45 encres de Dimitri Szabó

- *La Fresque* suivi de *La Trêve et autres poèmes mystiques*, poésie, Obsidiana Press, 2009

- *Où la fleur affleure,* poèmes et gravures de Corinne Leforestier, livre d'artiste, Les éditions libres de la cascade aux infinies questions, mai 2009

- *Demeure hors néant*, poèmes, Obsidiana Press, 2009

- *Entropie,* avec des encres de Dimitri Szabó, avril 2008

- *Fraternidad* (en castellano), Obsidiana Press, Plaquettes de Poesia, 2008

- *Le Don* (en français), Obsidiana Press, Plaquettes de Poesia, 2008

- *Variations* (en français et trilingue), éditions Textes et Prétextes, 2008

- *Miniatures : Parcelles d'un paradis inavouable*, livre d'artiste de Corinne Leforestier, 2008

- *Syncopes*, Textes et Prétextes, 2007

- *Dicha de lo dicho* (partition de Ioannis Kourtis), Éd. Eurochoral, 2007

- *Herbier de garrigue* (hors commerce – épuisé), 2006

- *Repères perdus*, le Buvard de l'Abîme, 2006

- *Páginas de invierno* (partition de Jean-Claude Wolff), Éd. Symétrie, 2006

- *Fragilité de cistes* (épuisé), 2005

- *Mis soledades / Mes solitudes*, Textes et Prétextes, 2005

- *Ojeada indolente / Coup d'œil nonchalant* (épuisé), Textes et Prétextes, 2004

- *Mini Poemas / Mini Poèmes* (épuisé), Textes et Prétextes, 2004

- *Abismo del corazón / Abîme du cœur* (épuisé), Textes et Prétextes, 2004

- *Ardor / Ardeur* (épuisé), Textes et Prétextes, 2004

- *Reinvendicación de la luz / Revendication de la lumière*, Louis Jean, 2003

- *Páginas de invierno / Pages d'hiver*, Louis

Jean, 2001

- *Charlas con el amor / Petites conversations avec l'amour*, (épuisé), Louis Jean, 2000,

- *La Fe : libreto de ópera / La Foi : livret d'opéra*, Louis Jean, 2000

- *Eres mi fantasma / Tu es mon fantasme*, Louis Jean, 2000

Poésie en revues

- *Fabulous way cinq poèmes dans Nueva Ola* décembre 2019 revue en espagnol et américain (Etats-Unis)

- *Triage* n°30, juin 2018, revue en français (France)

- *Paradoja* n°19, décembre 2015, revue en espagnol (Etats-Unis)

- *Sans titre*, deux poèmes en français et en italien (traducteurs : Franco Blandino et Gemma Francone), revue Margutte (Italie), novembre 2014

- *Letras TRL* N°62, septembre 2013, revue en espagnol (Espagne)

- *Emigrantskaïa Lira* N°2, 2013, revue en russe (Belgique)

- *Paradoja* n°15, janvier 2013, revue en espagnol (États-Unis)

- *The Refined Savage Poetry Review* n°6 janvier 2009, TRS Poetry Review, revue de poésie en anglais, États-Unis.

- *Paradoja* n°13 août 2008, revue en espagnol. États-Unis

- *Arcoiris* n°27 décembre 2008, Arcoiris, revue de création bilingue espagnol / français – Toulon, France

- *Le Capital des mots*, revue de poésie, n°8, juin 2008, Lecapitaldesmots, France

- *Arcoiris*, revue de création littéraire bilingue, n° 26, 2007, Arcoiris, France

- *Oglinda literara*, revue littéraire (traduction des poèmes en roumain par Ioana Trica), 2007, Roumanie

- *Sans titre*, poèmes publiés dans L'éveil du myosotis, anthologie dirigée par Jean-Pierre Béchu, Les éditions du net, Suresnes (France), 2014

- *Sans titre*, Terre de poètes, terre de paix, anthologie des poètes du monde sur la paix dirigée par Jean-Claude Awono, 2007 – Ifrikya, Cameroun

Poésie en anthologies

- *Sans titres*, Cinq poèmes publiés dans l'Agenda Poetas del Mundo, 2017, Chili

- *Sans titre*, Poème publié dans Les Poètes, L'Eau et le Feu, anthologie dirigée par Jean-Pierre Béchu et Marguerite Chamon, Les éditions du net, 2017 Suresnes, France,

- *Sans titre*, Poèmes publié dans l'Agenda Poetas del Mundo, 2016, Chili

- *Sans titre*, Poèmes publié dans l'Agenda Poetas del Mundo, 2015, Chili

- *Sans titre*, poème publié dans Voir feuille jointe. 12 plasticiens / 12 poètes, 2015, Octon, France,

- *The wide space on us*, 60 poèmes publiés dans The Wings of Poesy, anthologie dirigée par Mandal Bijoy Beg, Holi, 2015, Inde

- *Sans titre*, anthologie dirigée par Lourdes Batista, Solo para locos 2, Etats-Unis, 2015

- *Sans titre*, poème publié dans Les poètes et le cosmique anthologie dirigée par Jean-Pierre Béchu et Marguerite Chamon, Les éditions du net, Suresnes, France, 2015

- *Sans titre*, poèmes publiés dans L'éveil du myosotis, anthologie dirigée par Jean-Pierre Béchu, Les éditions du net, Suresnes (France), 2014

- *Sans titre*, Terre de poètes, terre de paix, anthologie des poètes du monde sur la paix dirigée par Jean-Claude Awono, 2007 – Ifrikya,

Cameroun

- Anthologie de la poésie francophone du début du XXIe siècle, 2007, Laurent Fels, Luxembourg

Poésie en catalogues d'exposition

- *Le créateur de calligraphie libre Shanshan Sun*, poème en français et en chinois (traducteur : Shanshan Sun), publié dans Energie : les œuvres de Shanshan Sun, livre d'art, China the Famous Press, Hong-Kong, 2015

- *Une voie singulière, Tempête de Shan*, poèmes en français et en chinois (traducteur : Shanshan Sun), publiés dans Peinture Taoïste de ShanShan, catalogue d'exposition, Beijing (Chine), juillet 2014

This First Edition of **Enigmatic sound**
by François Szabó was printed
in the United States of America in February
of 2020.

Obsidiana Press

obsidianapress.net
info@obsidianapress.net
oplibros@aol.com